llama llama home with mama

Anna Dewdney

VIKING
An Imprint of Penguin Group (USA) Inc.

llama llama home with mama

Anna Dewdney

VIKING

An Imprint of Penguin Group (USA) Inc.

Llama Llama, morning light.
Feeling yucky, just not right.

Down to breakfast.
Tiny sneeze.

Sniffle, snuffle.
Tissues, please!

Llama's head
is feeling hot.

Llama's throat
is hurting **lots.**

Achy, fever, stuffy head . . .
Llama Llama, back to bed.

Time to rest.
No school today.

Mama Llama
brings a tray.

Fruity medicine tastes **yucky!**
Llama Llama's throat feels gucky.

Look around. Not much to do.
Trucks are boring. Tractors, too.

Make a tunnel for a train?

Llama Llama, fuzzy brain.

Mama Llama gets a book.
Have a listen.
Take a look.

Heavy eyelids. Drippy nose.
Llama Llama starts to **doze.**

Up again and feeling better.

Draw some pictures.
Make some letters.

Llama wants a sandwich, please!
Mama Llama starts to sneeze.

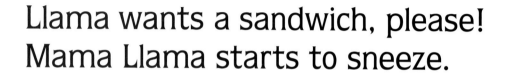

Lunch is over. Time for toys!
Mama's head does not like noise.

Mama makes a big **ah-choo!**

Llama's out of things to do.

Uh oh! Mama's throat is sore.

Being sick is such a **bore.**

Mama coughs,

and Llama yawns. . . .

How long can this day go on?

Mama shnortles, hacks, and wheezes.

Llama Llama's
sick of sneezes!

Soggy tissues,
gobs of guck.
Sniffing,
snorting,

Llama Llama, red pajama,
sick and bored, at home with Mama.

WAIT! Llama Llama knows what's best.

Mama Llama
needs a **rest!**

Get more tissues.

Bring a cup.

Fluff a comfy pillow up.

What else could Mama Llama need?

How about some **books** to read?

Just the thing for Llama Llama,
sick at home . . .

but with his mama.

For Ledlie and Leighton,
who love to stay home with their mama

VIKING
Published by Penguin Group
Penguin Young Readers Group, 345 Hudson Street, New York, New York 10014, U.S.A.
Penguin Group (Canada), 90 Eglinton Avenue East, Suite 700, Toronto, Ontario, Canada M4P 2Y3
(a division of Pearson Penguin Canada Inc.)
Penguin Books Ltd, 80 Strand, London WC2R 0RL, England

Penguin Books Ltd, Registered Offices: 80 Strand, London WC2R 0RL, England

First published in 2011 by Viking, a division of Penguin Young Readers Group

1 3 5 7 9 10 8 6 4 2

LIBRARY OF CONGRESS CATALOGING-IN-PUBLICATION
Dewdney, Anna.
Llama Llama home with Mama / by Anna Dewdney.
p. cm.
Summary: Llama Llama's mother takes good care of him when he has to stay home
from school because he is sick, but when Mama Llama begins to feel sick, too,
Llama Llama knows how to take care of her.
ISBN 978-0-670-01232-9 (hardcover)
Special Markets ISBN 978-0-670-78487-5 Not for resale
[1. Stories in rhyme. 2. Sick—Fiction. 3. Mother and child—Fiction. 4. Llamas—Fiction.] I. Title.
PZ8.3.D498Lj 2011
[E]—dc22
2011004910

Manufactured in China   Set in ITC Quorum

This Imagination Library edition is published by Penguin Group (USA), a Pearson
company, exclusively for Dolly Parton's Imagination Library, a not-for-profit
program designed to inspire a love of reading and learning, sponsored in part by The
Dollywood Foundation. Penguin's trade editions of this work are available wherever
books are sold.